READING CORNER

Poppy's Pancake Day

A humorous
rhyming story

This edition first published in 2010 by
Sea-to-Sea Publications
Distributed by Black Rabbit Books
P.O. Box 3263, Mankato, Minnesota 56002

Text © Sue Graves 2006, 2010
Illustration © Jane Eccles 2006

Printed in USA

Library of Congress Cataloging-in-Publication Data

Graves, Sue.
  Poppy's pancake day / written by Sue Graves ; illustrated by Jane Eccles.
      p. cm. -- (Reading corner)
  Summary: Dad and Poppy try to make a pancake for Mom who is sick in bed.
  ISBN 978-1-59771-244-6 (hardcover)
  [1. Stories in rhyme. 2. Family life--Fiction. 3. Pancakes, waffles, etc.--Fiction. 4.
Cookery--Fiction. 5. Sick--Fiction.] I. Eccles, Jane, ill. II. Title.
  PZ8.3.G7426Po 2010
  [E]--dc22
                            2008050450

9 8 7 6 5 4 3 2

Published by arrangement with the Watts Publishing Group Ltd., London

Series Editor: Jackie Hamley
Series Advisors: Dr. Linda Gambrell, Dr. Barrie Wade, Dr. Hilary Minns
Series Designer: Peter Scoulding

For my beautiful granddaughter, Isabelle—S.G.

Poppy's
Pancake Day

Written by
Sue Graves

Illustrated by
Jane Eccles

SEA-TO-SEA
Mankato Collingwood London

Sue Graves
"My family loves pancakes, but no one is very good at tossing them. Have you ever made pancakes?"

Jane Eccles
"I'm pretty good at making pancakes—I'm not as messy as Poppy anyway! I especially love drawing animals."

Mom was feeling sickly.

She felt faint and very ill.

"I think I'll go to bed," she said.

"I must have caught a chill."

Poppy made her cups of tea.

Dad bought a magazine.

But Mom just sat there sneezing,
and looking rather green.

"Poor Mom could do with cheering up," Dad said. "She looks so pasty.

Why don't we try to make her smile

by cooking something tasty?"

Poppy looked at recipes to
see what she could find.

There were lots of pies and pastries,

and cakes of every kind.

"Oh dear!" said Dad. "Those look too hard

Let's make something easy.

What about a sandwich...

...or toast that's thick and cheesy?"

"Pancakes are her favorite food,"
said Poppy with a smile.

"We could make lots of different ones
and stack them in a pile."

So Dad got eggs and butter;

Poppy flour and jam.

Then she got out the weighing scales
while Dad looked for the pan.

Poppy whisked the mixture.

She turned the mixer high.

The pancake mix spun around so
fast it hit Dad in the eye!

Soon the mix was ready.

"Time to cook them now," Dad said.

"Mom is going to love them.
She can eat them up in bed."

Dad poured the mixture in the pan, then tossed it in the air.

The pancake landed with a plop...

...on top of Poppy's hair!

"My turn now," said Poppy.

She gave the pan a flip.

The pancake shot up skywards,

and then began to tip...

...It hovered for a moment...

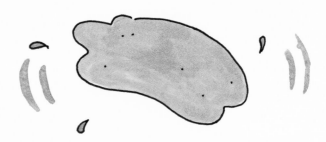

...and then spun around and
around.

And with a very noisy splat,

it landed on the ground.

So Dad and Poppy mopped the floor and cleaned up all the mess.

Then went to see how Mom felt,

now that she had had a rest.

"I'm feeling better now," said Mom.

"Why look, it's half past three.

Let's go and make some pancakes as a special treat. Shall we?"

Notes for parents and teachers

READING CORNER has been structured to provide maximum support for new readers. The stories may be used by adults for sharing with young children. Primarily, however, the stories are designed for newly independent readers, whether they are reading these books in bed at night, or in the reading corner at school or in the library.

Starting to read alone can be a daunting prospect. READING CORNER helps by providing visual support and repeating words and phrases, while making reading enjoyable. These books will develop confidence in the new reader, and encourage a love of reading that will last a lifetime.

If you are reading this book with a child, here are a few tips:

1. Make reading fun. Choose a time to read when you and the child are relaxed and have time to share the story.

2. Encourage children to reread the story, and to retell the story in their own words, using the illustrations to remind them what has happened.

3. Give praise. Remember that small mistakes need not always be corrected.

READING CORNER covers three grades of early reading ability, with three levels at each grade. Each level has a certain number of words per story, indicated by the number of bars on the spine of the book, to allow you to choose the right book for a young reader:

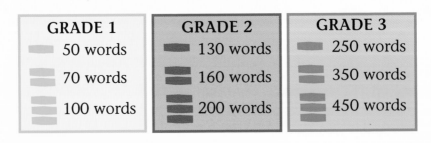

GRADE 1	GRADE 2	GRADE 3
50 words	130 words	250 words
70 words	160 words	350 words
100 words	200 words	450 words